The Adventures of Scooter and Smack

Darlien Simos

The Adventures of Scooter and Smack

Copyright ©2021 by Darlien Simos

All rights reserved.
No part of this book may be reproduced, scanned, or distributed in any printed or electronic form without express permission from the author.

ISBN: 978-1-939237-81-1

Illustrated by: Zoe Radford

Published by Suncoast Digital Press, Inc.
Sarasota, Florida, USA

Contents

Scooter and Smack & The Ice Cream Truck . 1

Scooter and Smack at The Beach 19

Scooter and Smack Make New Friends...... 33

Scooter and Smack & The Rainy Day 51

Scooter and Smack Save The Baby Bird 63

About the Author 75

Dedication

This book is dedicated to my family, and the hours we have enjoyed reading similar books, that would teach the love of reading, through rhyme, sequence, and adventure!

Scooter and Smack
&
The Ice Cream Truck

I know a little dog who is black-spotted
and white from his head to his toes,
with a little brown patch on his nose.

His name is Scooter.

His best friend is Smack—a squirrel, believe it or not.

He is kind of a frisky little fellow who would smack his lips whenever he was in trouble.

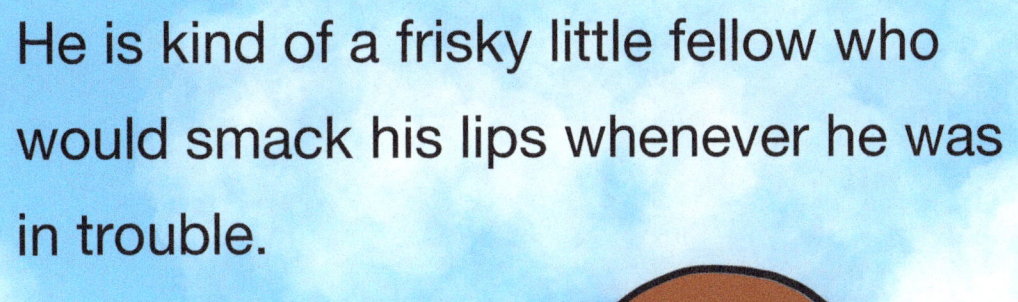

All over town went Scooter and Smack.

Where will they go today?

Let's follow them on their way.

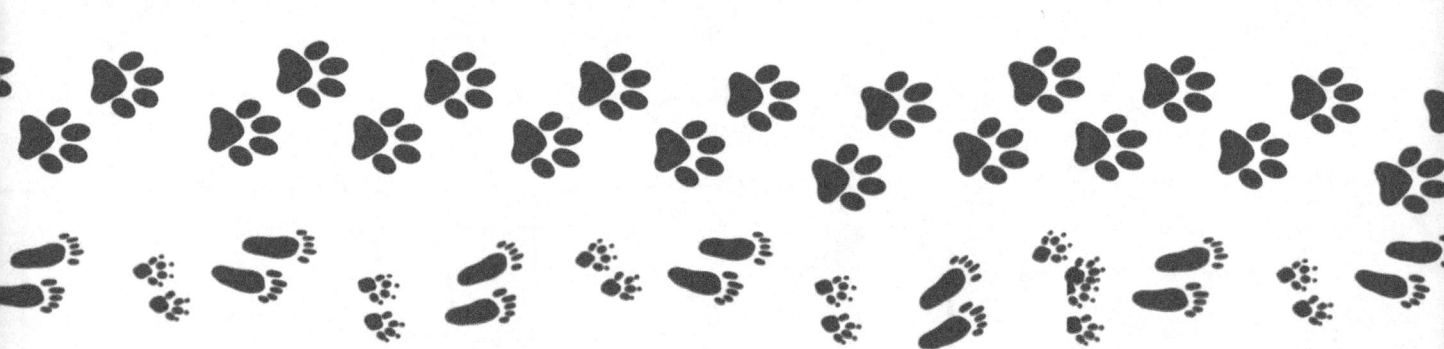

Look up ahead!

There's a boy with an ice cream cone.

Scooter was hot and so was Smack—a nice lick of ice cream would make a good snack.

But where did it come from?

Could it be from that truck driving up ahead on the road with something yummy on top?

Smack said, "I bet that it's full of delicious cold ice cream," and Scooter agreed.

Together they followed that truck with speed!

When they got closer, Smack jumped on top, smacking his lips because he felt afraid.

"Smack!" Scooter yelled, "Get down from there.

We'll find another way to get our ice cream to share."

Smack had another idea in his head,
but before he could do it,
the traffic light turned red.

Smack flew onto the front of the truck.

Now what was he going to do?

He was kind of stuck.

The driver looked up. "Hey, where did you come from, poor little squirrel?

Let me help you. Would you like a swirl?

He helped Smack off and gave him a nice cold treat!

Scooter came around to see his friend eat.

"Smack, are you alright?"
Smack looked at Scooter with a big smile on his face.

Seeing the two friends together, the driver said, "Let me give your friend a treat, too, on this very hot day."

And that is how Scooter and Smack got their ice cream that day!

It was not that easy, by the way.

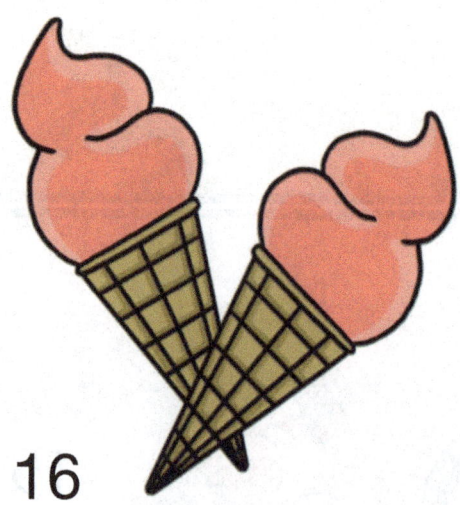

But for Scooter and Smack, it worked out just fine!

Tomorrow will bring another adventure to find.

Scooter and Smack
At the Beach

For Scooter and Smack,
there is nothing like a day at the beach
to lie around and do nothing.

But that is not always so…

"Smack!" yelled Scooter.

"What's that on your toe?"

"Yikes!" screamed Smack.

"That crab thinks I'm lunch!

Get it off before it starts to munch!"

"Let's build a sandcastle
'cause that's fun to do."

"Let's make it big!

Let's make two!"

"Not too close to the water you know,
or that crab might come back
and bite my toe!"

Scooter said, "Let's jump on in and get wet and swim, swim, swim," and off they went.

"Watch out for those waves."

Splish, splash, splish.

Where is Smack now?

He has climbed up on top of that sea turtle somehow.

Come back, Smack!" Scooter yelled.

"Get off of him, you're out too far, you're out too deep, come on in and use your feet."

"Kick that water up and down, before you know it, you'll be back on the ground!" Scooter said.

"I'm glad you're back," and Smack agreed, his lips stopped smacking and he went snacking.

"Let's get something to eat," he said with a grin.

"I am hungry like a sea turtle!" Scooter laughed.

"Oh, Smack, a day at the beach with you to lie around and do nothing?"

"Well…maybe next time, I'm exhausted!" exclaimed Scooter.

"After we eat, Let's go home and rest our feet."

As much fun as it is at the beach, no matter where we roam, there's no place like home."

Scooter and Smack Make New Friends

Today began like any other, with Scooter and Smack playing games with each other.

"You're it!" said Scooter. "No, you're it!" said Smack.

"Now come back here so I can get you back!"

They played all day and into the night.

They met some new friends that made everything just right.

Scamper, a furry little raccoon, who joined in on the fun before noon, and Hopper the frog, they met at the pond catching some flies for lunch while sitting on a log.

Suddenly, they all heard a noise wisping through the breeze. "Please, help me!" the tiny voice said.

It was a little mouse, stuck in the berry bush up ahead!

I'll help you!" called Smack, without thinking what to do,

And he started to jump in, too!

"Wait!" Scooter yelled, "don't jump into that thorn bush!" but Smack was in a rush!

Ouch, ouch!" yelped Smack as he came back out, and said, "let's just think of a way we can all help."

Listening from above was a wise old owl, waking up from his daytime nap.

"Why don't you use that old fishing pole that someone left in the old fishing hole?"

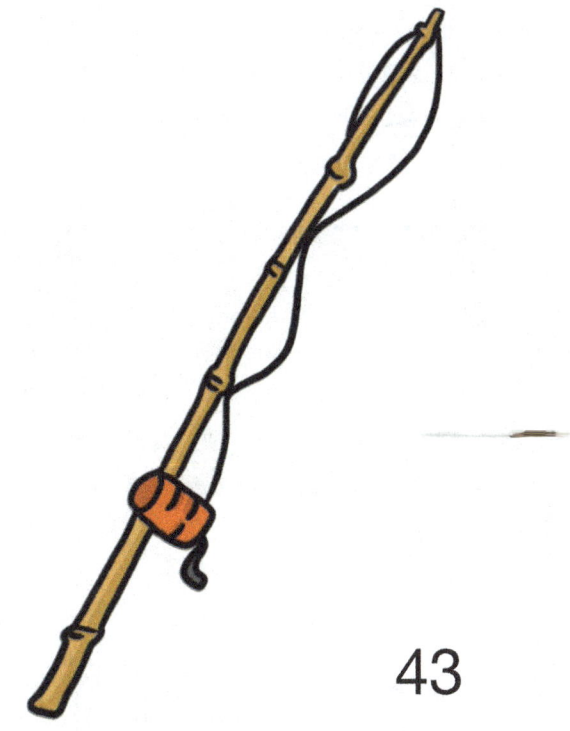

Scamper grabbed the pole, saying, "What good luck!" He pushed the end to where the little mouse was stuck.

The job was done and the friends all cheered!

The mouse was now safe from the bush he had feared.

Before they went home, they could not resist all of those berries that they had sniffed.

They carefully plucked them one by one and had a berry feast until there were none.

Then they said "good-bye" and headed home.

Their bellies were full and it was time to say thank you to all, for the great team-work today.

Working together is the better way.

Scooter and Smack
And the Rainy Day

Today began as a very wet, rainy day.

The sun was not out, there was nothing to play—all they could do was sit and watch the rain go drip, drop, drip.

"What should we do?" asked a very bored Scooter.

"I know, let's run and look for frogs and bugs and play all day and roll in the mud!"

So, that's what they did, exploring the land, rolling in every puddle they found was just grand!

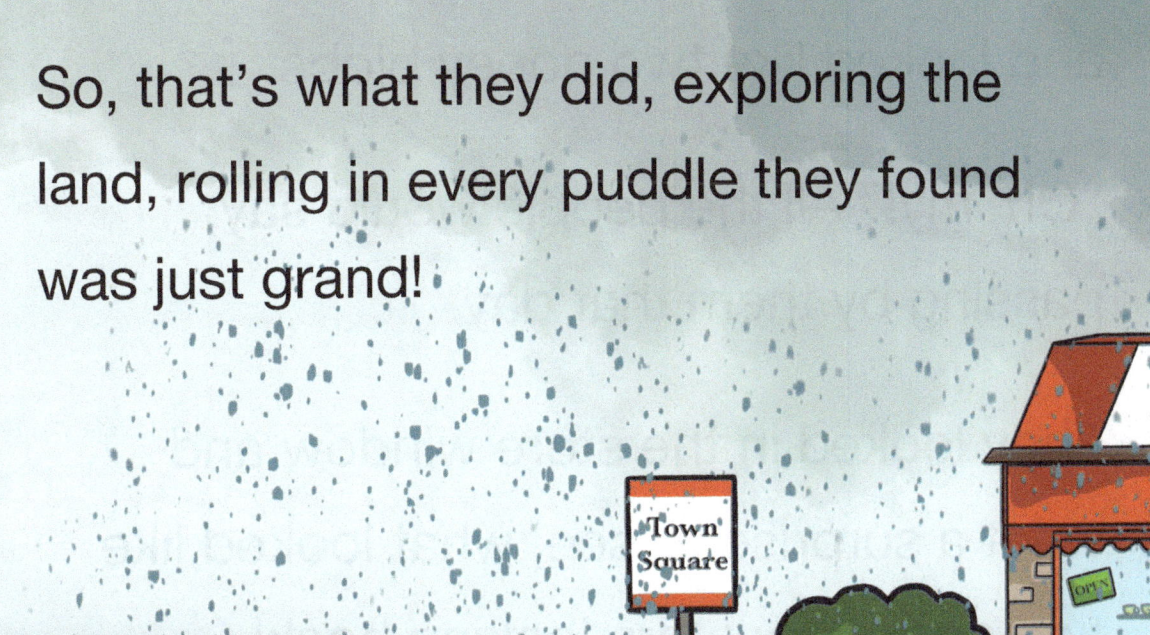

The sun came out and they started to dry and looked like two gooey blobs.

"Oh, my!" All the people would say, passing by them that day.

They looked in the store window and what a surprise to see, what looked like two scary monsters looking back!

Smack was smacking his lips as he shook…

"Smack!" called Scooter, "that's us in there, that's how we look!"

Just their luck, across the street was a firehouse, next to Doggie Treats, their favorite place!

This plan of theirs would get them clean and a treat to go would complete this day that had started out so drab and gray.

They ran across and took the hose and sprayed each other from their head to toes.

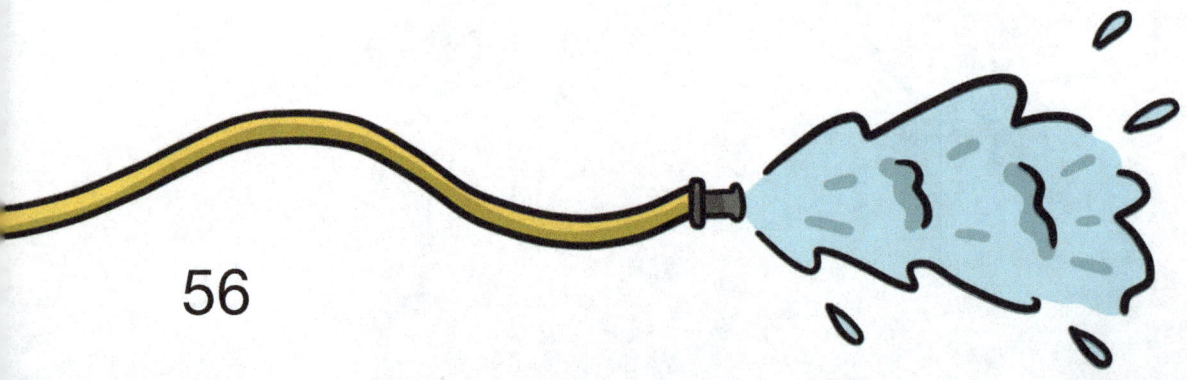

Nice and clean was not easy to be—that mud was stuck on them like sap on a tree.

Their plan was working out better than they hoped. The Doggie Treat truck just drove up the slope!

"Two doggie treats, please," they would say if they talked—they barked at the man until he exclaimed, "Stop!"

"Here you go, puppies, now run off and play," and they did run all the way home. What a day!

"It's nice to be back home to eat our treat," said Scooter, as he wondered what will happen the next time they meet up with a rainy day once again.

There are so many things you can do, by yourself or with a friend!

Scooter and Smack Save the Baby Bird

One spring day, Scooter and Smack were walking down the road by the railroad track, when Scooter yelled out, "Hey, Smack, look what I found!"

A baby bird had fallen to the ground.

"There is the nest up in that tree, I wonder where his mother could be!"

"We must get help for that bird right away, so I will find someone and bring them—you stay!"

While Scooter was gone, Smack had quite a time keeping that baby bird safe and sublime.

He began to smack his lips, which he did in fear.

Then he stopped—his job right now was to protect the baby bird who was near.

"Don't be sad, little bird," he would say, and sing to it, dance for it, and laugh with it all day.

The little bird wanted to stay with Smack, but Smack said, "Oh, no!" and that was that.

Then he saw Scooter coming down the road with Police Officer Stan, a kind fellow, tall, dark, and tan.

He picked up the bird, put him back in the nest, said "Good job!" and gave the pals his best…two badges, that is.

He said Scooter and Smack were heroes that day, waved goodbye and was on his way!

They saved the baby bird and were happy to say, helping someone in need is the best way!

The End

About the Author

Working with elementary-aged children is a passion of Darlien Simos. When she is not teaching, she spends her time with her family.

She is married to her husband, Sotirios, and they have four children, Paul, Jonathan, Alexander and Elena.

Please visit:
www.ScooterandSmack.com

Made in the USA
Las Vegas, NV
25 June 2023